Millions of Americans remember Dick and Jane (and Sally and Spot too!). The little stories with their simple vocabulary words and warmly rendered illustrations were a hallmark of American education in the 1950s and 1960s.

But the first Dick and Jane stories actually appeared much earlier—in the Scott Foresman Elson Basic Reader Pre-Primer, copyright 1930. These books featured short, upbeat, and highly readable stories for children. The pages were filled with colorful characters and large, easy-to-read Century Schoolbook typeface. There were fun adventures around every corner of Dick and Jane's world.

Generations of American children learned to read with Dick and Jane, and many still cherish the memory of reading the simple stories on their own. Today, Pearson Scott Foresman remains committed to helping all children learn to read—and love to read. As part of Pearson Education, the world's largest educational publisher, Pearson Scott Foresman is honored to reissue these classic Dick and Jane stories, with Grosset & Dunlap, a division of Penguin Young Readers Group. Reading has always been at the heart of everything we do, and we sincerely hope that reading is an important part of your life too.

Dick and Jane is a registered trademark of Addison-Wesley Educational Publishers, Inc. From GUESS WHO. Copyright © 1951 by Scott Foresman and Company, copyright renewed 1979. All rights reserved. Published in 2003 by Grosset & Dunlap, a division of Penguin Young Readers Group, 345 Hudson Street, New York, NY, 10014. GROSSET & DUNLAP is a trademark of Penguin Group (USA) Inc. Published simultaneously in Canada. Printed in the U.S.A.

Library of Congress Cataloging-in-Publication Data

Guess who.
    p. cm. — (Read with Dick and Jane ; 4)
Summary: A collection of reissued stories with simple vocabulary featuring Dick, Jane, and other familiar characters.
  ISBN 0-448-43403-2 (pbk.) — ISBN 0-448-43415-6 (hardcover)
  1. Readers (Primary) [1. Readers.] I. Series.
  PE1119.G84 2003
  428.6—dc22   2003016957

ISBN 0-448-43403-2 (pbk)   F G H I J

ISBN 0-448-43415-6 (GB)   B C D E F G H I J

Read with
Dick and Jane

Guess Who

GROSSET & DUNLAP • NEW YORK

Who Can Work?

Dick said, "See me work.
I can help Father.
I can get something.
Something for Father."

Dick said, "Look Father.
Jane plays and plays.
You and Mother work.
And I work.
Jane can not work.
Jane is a little baby."

Father said, "Oh, Dick.
Jane is not a baby."

Jane said, "See me now.

I can do something.

See me work.

I can help Mother.

See what I can do.

Sally is a baby.

Sally can not work."

Mother said, "Oh, my.
Sally is not here.
Who can find Sally?"

Sally said, "Look, Mother.
See me in my little house.
I can work.
And Spot and Puff can work.
We can make a house.
A funny little house."

Find My Ball

Sally said, "I want my ball.
My pretty yellow ball.
Who can find it for me?"

Jane said, "Here is a ball.
See this blue ball, Sally.
Do you want this ball?"

Sally said, "I want my ball.
My ball is yellow.
It is a big, pretty ball.
And it is in this house.
Help me find it."

"It is not here," said Dick.

Sally said, "Where is my ball?
It is in this house.
Where, oh, where is it?"

"It is not here," said Dick.
"Not down here, Sally."

Sally said, "Oh, Spot.
Do you see my ball?
Where is it, Spot?
Go and get it."

Sally said, "Oh, Jane.

Look up.

Look up.

See where my ball is.

Oh, oh, oh.

Dick looks down.

Little Spot looks up.

And Spot finds my ball.

My pretty yellow ball."

A Big Red Car

Dick said, "Away I go.
Away in my big red car.
See me go, Sally."

Sally said, "I want a car.
Make two cars, Dick.
A car for you.
And a car for me.
Make two cars."

Dick said, "Oh, Sally.
You can come in my car.
In my big red car."

"I want a car," said Sally.
"Make one for me, Dick.
A little one for me."

Dick said, "Look, Sally.
I can do something.
See what I can do.
I can make a big, big car.
Two can get in this car now."

Dick said, "Here, Sally.
This will look pretty in my car.
I will make it go up for you.
See it go up, up, up.
Now get in my car."

"Away we go," said Sally.
"Away, away in a big red car."

Who Will Jump?

Dick said, "Look, Sally.
Do you see this?
Come with me.
You will see something funny."

Sally said, "Oh, Dick.

I see what you want to do.

You want to make me jump.

Oh, oh.

You want to make me jump."

Dick said, "Not you, Sally.

I want to find Jane.

I want to make Jane jump."

Sally said, "I see Jane.

Jane is in the house.

Oh, oh.

I want to go in the house.

I want to see Jane jump."

"Come with me," said Dick.

"Come in the house with me.

You will see something funny.

You will see Jane jump."

Dick said, "Now look, Sally.

Now you will see Jane jump.

One . . . Two . . ."

"Three," said Sally.

"One, two, three.

See Dick jump."

I See You

Jane said, "Come with me, Sally.
Come to the house with me.
Dick will not look here.
Not in the house.
Dick will not find you here."

Dick said, "Oh, oh.

I see something blue.

I can guess where Jane is.

One, two, three for Jane.

I see you, Jane.

One, two, three for you.

"Come with me, Puff.

We want to find Sally now.

Where, oh, where is Sally?"

Dick said, "Oh, oh.

I see something yellow.

I can guess where Sally is.

One, two, three for Sally.

I see Sally with Jane.

One, two, three for Sally.

"Now, little Puff.

Do you want to come with me?

We will get Jane and Sally."

Jane said, "One, two, three.
One, two, three for me.
And one, two, three for Sally.
Sally is with me."

Dick said, "Oh, funny me.
This is something yellow.
It is not Sally.
And this is something blue.
It is not Jane."

Guess Who

Sally said, "See the cars.
See the cars go up, up, up.
One, two, three.
Three little yellow cars."

Father said, "Oh, Baby Sally.
You can not play here.
This is where we work.
Here is a ball.
Run and play with the ball."

Mother said, "Spot, Spot.
Go to the house.
You can not play here.
Come with me to the house."

Jane said, "Come here, Dick.
Oh, come here.
Guess what I see.
Guess what Spot can make."

Sally said, "Oh, pretty, pretty.
Spot can make something pretty.
I can do what Spot can do.
I can make something pretty."

Jane said, "Oh, Father.
I want to do it."

Father said, "Come, Dick.
You and Jane can do it.
And here is little Puff.
I will help Puff do it."

Dick said, "Look, Mother.
See what we can make.
Guess who this is."

"Guess who this is," said Jane.

"Guess who this is," said Sally.
"And see the two little ones.
Guess who.
Guess who."